HAWKEYE JOINS

Based on the Marvel
comic book series
The Mighty Avengers
Adapted by Tomas Palacios
Illustrated by Mike Norton
and Brian Miller

Published by Marvel Press, an
imprint of Disney Book Group.
No part of this book may be
reproduced or transmitted in
any form or by any means,
electronic or mechanical, including
photocopying, recording, or by any
information storage and retrieval
system, without written permission
from the publisher.

For information address Marvel
Press, 114 Fifth Avenue, New York,
New York 10011-5690.
Printed in the United States of
America
First Edition
1 3 5 7 9 10 8 6 4 2
G658-7729-4-12061
ISBN 978-1-4231-4277-5

marvelkids.com

MARVEL
New York

Clint Barton and his brother, Barney, grew up in an orphanage. They kept busy by making Super Hero costumes and reading about Wild West adventures.

When they were old enough, they left the orphanage, excited to explore the world. One day, **they came upon a large tent.** They heard noises coming from within, but they weren't sure what was going on. . . .

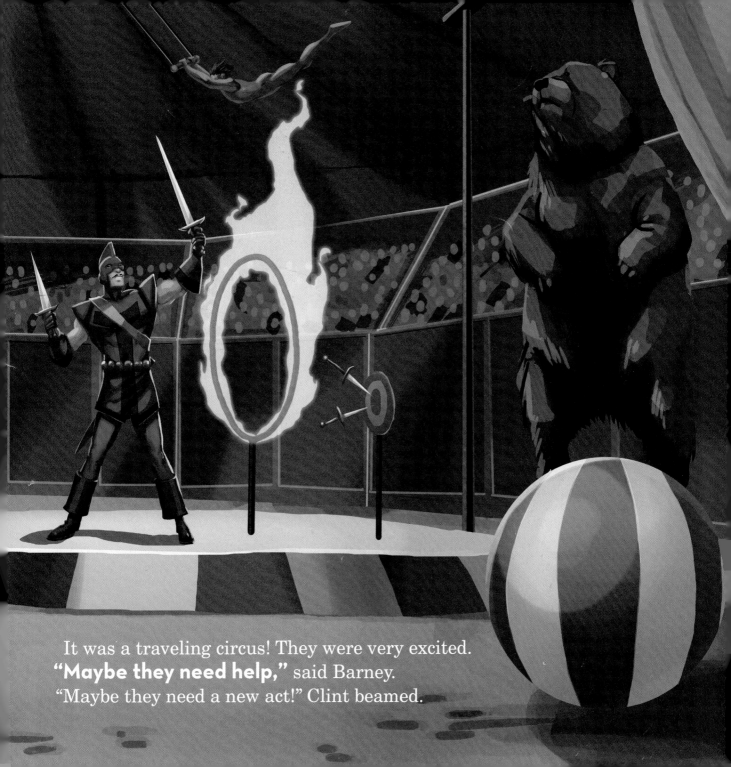

It was a traveling circus! They were very excited.
"Maybe they need help," said Barney.
"Maybe they need a new act!" Clint beamed.

"Maybe we need both," said a voice. "I'm **the Swordsman,** and this is the world-famous Carson Carnival of Traveling Wonders! We could use some help around here. Interested?"

The brothers were thrilled! **"Yes, we are!"** they said together.

The brothers quickly learned many jobs around the circus. Barney enjoyed helping out behind the curtain.

But Clint enjoyed being in *front* of the curtain! He was especially good with the bow and arrow.

Clint practiced...and practiced...

He got better...and better...

Until one day...

Clint became a headlining act! Known as **Hawkeye, the World's Greatest Marksman**, Clint was *the* star performer! The circus was making lots of money. So much, in fact, someone wanted to take some....

One night, after a sold-out show, Hawkeye was surprised to find the box office still open. He went to take a look. He was shocked to see it was the Swordsman—**stealing money!**

"What are you doing?" asked Hawkeye.

"Out of my way, kid!" The Swordsman said as he began to run off. Hawkeye aimed his bow and arrow, but he couldn't bring himself to hurt his mentor.

Several performers heard the noise. They were upset Clint failed to stop the Swordsman. They didn't want him in their circus anymore.

Months later, Hawkeye had taken his act to a beachfront carnival. One day, he **heard an explosion**.

People were in danger! *Someone needs to help them*, Hawkeye thought.

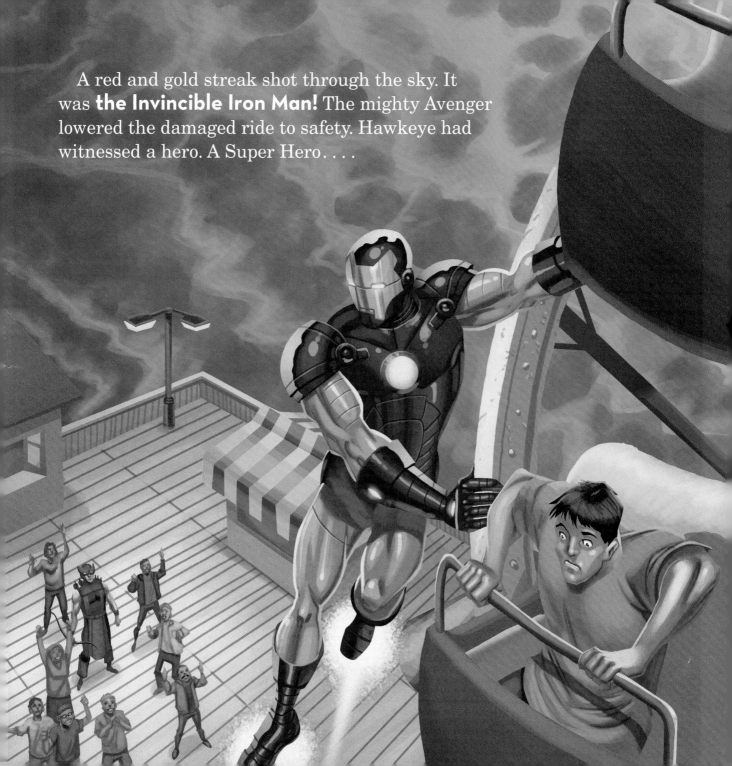

A red and gold streak shot through the sky. It was **the Invincible Iron Man!** The mighty Avenger lowered the damaged ride to safety. Hawkeye had witnessed a hero. A Super Hero. . . .

That night, Clint realized that he could help protect the innocent, just like Iron Man. He raced home and **began working on a new costume**.

Using tricks he learned from performers in the circus, Clint made a large variety of special arrows.

"Time for the world to meet **Hawkeye!**" he said.

As Hawkeye was on the lookout, he saw someone robbing the local jewelry store. Hawkeye appeared, and the thief dropped the jewels and fled!

Suddenly, a police car pulled up behind Hawkeye!

"Put your hands up!" they yelled to Hawkeye.

Oh no, he thought. *They think I stole the jewels!*

Hawkeye tried to escape, but
Iron Man appeared!
"So you like to steal?" he said.
"Wait, I'm innocent!"
cried Hawkeye.
"I hear that a lot,"
joked Iron Man.

Iron Man fired a **repulsor blast** at Hawkeye. But Hawkeye was fast! He quickly dodged the blast and fired an arrow at Iron Man!

"You think you can stop me with an arrow?" Iron Man said. But when he tried to remove the arrow, it exploded in a **cloud of smoke!**

"Not just an arrow," Hawkeye yelled. An electric net sprung from the arrow, trapping Iron Man. **"I don't want to fight you!"** Hawkeye said, freeing Iron Man from the net. "I was trying to stop the thief."

"I believe you," Iron Man said, as he got to his feet. "I just heard over my armor's radio that the thief was caught."

Hawkeye put out his hand, **"The name is Hawkeye."**

"They call me Iron Man," the armored Avenger said, shaking it. And behind you..."

"Are the Mighty Avengers!"

"Wow!" Hawkeye said. "I've heard of you! Thor, Hulk, Ant-Man, Wasp, Captain America."

"And Hawkeye," said Iron Man. "I think your unique skills will be a great help to us."

Hawkeye had never been happier. From that day forth, Hawkeye was a member of the Mighty Avengers. His dream had finally come true. **He was a Super Hero!**